Luke went to lie on his bed and stare up at the football posters on the ceiling while he listened to the radio. Something the commentator was saying, however, suddenly made him pay extra attention.

'The player-manager has performed wonders. It's been a one-man show. He's taken the game by the scruff of the neck and given it a good shake, as if to say: "This is my team and I'll do what I like. I'm the boss!"'

'That's it!' exclaimed Luke, jumping off the bed in excitement. 'Why didn't I think of that before? Who cares if Frosty doesn't want me? I can form my own team to play in the Sunday League – and pick myself to play centre-forward every week!'

Find out how Luke forms his team in this terrific introductory title to the popular and bestselling *Soccer Mad* series, already published by Corgi Yearling Books.

Also available by Rob Childs:

Published by Corgi Yearling Books

Soccer Mad series
SOCCER MAD
ALL GOALIES ARE CRAZY
FOOTBALL DAFT
FOOTBALL FLUKES

Sandford series
SOCCER AT SANDFORD
SANDFORD ON TOUR

Published by Young Corgi Books

THE BIG BREAK
THE BIG CHANCE
THE BIG CLASH
THE BIG DAY
THE BIG FREEZE
THE BIG GAME
THE BIG GOAL
THE BIG KICK
THE BIG MATCH
THE BIG PRIZE
THE BIG STAR
THE BIG WIN
THE BIG FOOTBALL COLLECTION
(three books-in-one)
THE BIG FOOTBALL FEAST
(three books-in-one)

For beginner readers, published by Corgi Pups:
GREAT SAVE!

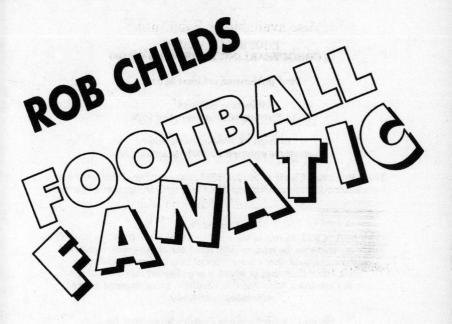

ROB CHILDS
FOOTBALL FANATIC

ILLUSTRATED BY
AIDAN POTTS

CORGI YEARLING BOOKS

FOOTBALL FANATIC
A CORGI YEARLING BOOK : 0 440 863600

First publication in Great Britain

PRINTING HISTORY
Corgi Yearling edition published 1998

Set in 12/15 pt Linotype Century Schoolbook by
Phoenix Typesetting, Ilkley, West Yorkshire

Corgi Yearling books are published by Transworld Publishers Ltd,
61–63 Uxbridge Road, Ealing, London W5 5SA,
in Australia by Transworld Publishers (Australia) Pty. Ltd,
15–25 Helles Avenue, Moorebank, NSW 2170,
and in New Zealand by Transworld Publishers (NZ) Ltd,
3 William Pickering Drive, Albany, Auckland.

Made and printed in Great Britain by
Cox & Wyman Ltd, Reading, Berkshire

*For all young football fans
and fanatics!*

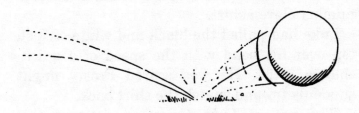

1   Penalty King

Luke Crawford clenched his fists and punched the air in delight.

'Yeeesss!'

The strangled cry escaped from his throat like the hiss of gas from a Bunsen burner. The noise startled a dog that was wandering across the pitch and it slunk off over the playing fields, tail between its legs.

The crowd of one man and his dog was reduced by fifty per cent.

'I've made it! I've actually gone and made it!'

This was no time to act cool. Luke didn't know how to in any case. At last he was included in the starting line-up for the Year 7 soccer team. Two players had failed to turn up for the Saturday morning fixture and 'Frosty' Winter, Swillsby Comprehensive's grouchy P.E. teacher, was forced to swallow hard and hand Luke the number eleven shirt.

Luke had pulled the black and white striped top over his head with the speed of a quick-change artist. He was scared Frosty might suddenly try and snatch the shirt back.

'The patient Luke Crawford deserves this opportunity to show what he can do. He's waited all season for this moment . . .'

The voice, trembling with barely suppressed excitement, belonged to Luke himself. He was pretending to be the match commentator, a role that he normally had to perform along the touch-line as a frustrated spectator or non-playing substitute. But not today. This time his running commentary would be in the thick of the action.

'Frosty Winter won't regret his decision. Luke is determined to prove he's worth his place in the side. He'll make sure this will be a game that the coach won't forget in a hurry . . .'

His biased commentary had never made a more accurate pre-match forecast. Frosty would have been prepared to pay a lot of money to any hypnotherapist who could guarantee that the events of the next hour could be erased from his memory.

Luke's first touch on his full debut for the Comp set the tone for what was to lie ahead. It wasn't a silky flick of the ball, but a clumsy clip of the heels of the Padley High School winger as he cut inside the area for a shot at goal.

'Penalty!' squealed all the Padley players in chorus.

Frosty's heart sank. As far as he was concerned – and he knew that some of the boys shared his jaundiced view on the subject – Luke

Crawford was a walking disaster on the soccer pitch. And the catastrophic effects were even worse when he *ran*.

As referee, Frosty could think up no excuse why he shouldn't blow his whistle and point to the penalty spot. So that's what he had to do.

The Comp captain grabbed Luke by the collar and yanked him away.

'What yer doing here, messing things up for us?' Matthew Clarke demanded. 'Get up on that wing and stay there – out of the way!'

'Only trying to help,' Luke protested feebly, pulling his prized shirt back straight. 'Just missed the ball, that's all.'

So did the goalkeeper. Sanjay Mistry dived the wrong way for the penalty and the ball looped into the opposite corner. He glared towards Luke and hoofed the ball upfield for the restart. His only consolation was to imagine it was the number eleven's head.

The one bit of sympathy Luke received came from cousin Jon, the Comp's leading scorer. 'Never mind, Luke,' Jon called over to him. 'Everybody makes mistakes.'

Matthew overheard the remark and seized upon it, twisting it to his own advantage. 'Yeah, but nobody makes as many as Loony Luke!'

Luke shrugged. Matthew was always calling him names, but he refused to be put off. He attended every soccer practice, the first one to be changed and ready to go out and work on his skills. That was perhaps just as well. He certainly needed more time on them than anybody else. And yet his only reward before this windy March morning had been a couple of brief – very brief – appearances as sub.

He sought solace in his commentary, which was suitably hushed. '*An unfortunate, mistimed challenge has put the Comp behind, but there's plenty of time left yet to put matters right. This may be just a friendly, but these two local rivals*

are mad keen to beat each other . . .'

Swillsby were soon 2–0 down, although no blame could be attached to Luke for the second goal. He hadn't been allowed near the ball for ten minutes. When it did finally drop at his feet in a goalmouth scramble, he swung at it wildly and the ball was still rising as it cleared the hedge.

Luke tried to ignore the jeers, mostly from his own team, and resumed his lonely patrol of the left touchline.

'Unlucky bobble there, just at the crucial moment, or Luke Crawford would have put the Comp back in the game,' murmured the blinkered commentary. *'If only they could get the ball out to their new winger more often, he'd be sure to give the slow Padley full-back the run around . . .'*

Luke was left to his own little world of fantasy football as the match swirled along without him. It didn't look much different to him than usual, apart from the fact that he was cutting a groove up and down the pitch one metre inside the touchline instead of outside it.

It *felt* different, though. It felt colder. He hadn't got his coat on.

By half-time he was freezing. 'Four–one, and I've hardly had a kick yet,' he muttered to Jon as

the players slouched towards Frosty to suffer the teacher's complaints. 'If nobody will pass to me, I might as well not be playing. You'd be better off with ten men.'

He paused so that Jon could at least deny it, but his cousin just grinned instead. 'Don't fret. I'll try and slip you the ball a few times second half. Got to remind Frosty you're still here.'

Luke brightened. 'Yeah, thanks, Johan. I'll remind him all right.'

Luke was a great student of football. Even though he would fail any practical exam on the pitch, he was world class in terms of his knowledge of the game. His bedroom was a soccer shrine, full of posters, pictures, videos, annuals and manuals. His personal hero was Johan Cruyff, the Ajax and Holland star of the 1970s, whom he rated even higher than the legendary Pele. To nickname his cousin Johan was praise indeed.

Jon lived up to such an accolade straight from the kick-off. Shaping to pass the ball out to Luke on the wing, the number eight kept it himself and caught the Padley defence by surprise and wrong-footed them for a second. It was all the time he needed. He swept through a gap his dummy had created and took on the

goalkeeper, Ravi, at speed.

Ravi was a teammate of both Jon and Matthew for Padley Panthers, a top division Sunday League outfit. He'd been boasting for weeks that neither of them would score against him, but this was the moment of truth.

Jon drew Ravi forward, committing him to make a dive at his feet, then whisked the ball away with a conjuror's skill. Now you see it, now you don't. The vanishing act ended with the ball somehow re-appearing in the net, leaving the bemused Ravi scratching his head as he lay on the ground. He had no idea how the trick had been done.

The Comp's hopes were raised for a short while, but came crashing down as soon as Luke took over centre stage. In its own way, Luke's solo performance was every bit as memorable as his cousin's piece of magic.

This time Jon made a fatal mistake. He didn't just look as if he was going to pass to Luke, he then went and did so. Luke immediately set off on a run – towards his own goal.

'Turn, turn!' screamed Matthew, but it was to no avail.

Luke couldn't turn, no matter how hard he tried. Two Padley players were snapping at his

ankles, herding him like a stray sheep back into home territory.

'Kick it out!' yelled Sanjay as Luke was driven into the penalty area.

Luke panicked. His feet were not very clever at obeying orders at the best of times and now they became tangled up. He tripped and sprawled full length on top of the ball, but at least he managed to save it from rolling loose for a corner. He was cradling it in his arms.

'Penalty!' It was a familiar appeal.

And only five minutes after this penalty was converted, Luke proceeded to give the kicker a further chance to practise his art. Sanjay had already fumbled a sloppy sixth goal into the net and was past caring when he saw Luke drifting back to lend a hand with the marking at a corner.

Luke lent both of them in fact. Fate unkindly decreed that the ball should find the number eleven in the crowded goalmouth. He was partly unsighted by other bodies when it suddenly loomed up in front of him at an awkward height. Luke didn't know whether to try and kick it, knee it, chest it or head the ball clear. He ended up catching it instead. The ball plopped into his stomach and he grabbed hold of it instinctively.

The cries of the Padley team were perfectly synchronized by now.

'Penalty!'

'Er, I think that's handball again, ref,' said their captain politely.

Frosty sighed with resignation. 'Aye, you're probably right, lad,' he replied, pointing once more to the spot.

'Accidental, honest,' claimed Luke, protesting his innocence as Matthew strode towards him menacingly.

'You're a total waste of space!' the captain snarled. 'Just hope you never get picked to play for us again.'

Frosty muttered something as well. Luke liked to believe it might have been 'Get ready, everybody.'

It was wishful thinking. He half-suspected what it really was.

'Over my dead body!'

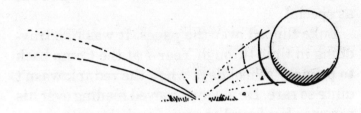

2   Do-It-Yourself

Sitting at his bedroom desk on the Saturday afternoon, the radio blaring out a match commentary, Luke wrote the score of the school game neatly into a little black notebook.

Comp 2 v 7 Padley High

He went on to record the date, the ground conditions, the names of the Comp's players in their team formation, 4–3–3, and the scorers, plus a brief match report. He failed to mention the reasons for all the penalties, apart from describing the referee's decisions as *harsh*.

He gazed in satisfaction at the name of

CRAWFORD, L., in capitals, next to Crawford, J. in the attack. It felt good to have used a red pen again in his meticulous soccer logbook. Most of the entries were in black ink, but his own appearances for the school deserved to stand out as special.

Luke flipped over the pages. It was like travelling in time through Year 7 at the Comp back to primary school days when the red ink wasn't quite so rare. He always enjoyed reading over his reports. He found the one describing the very first goal he scored for Swillsby Primary.

'Luke Crawford took his time, picked his spot and slotted the ball coolly past the helpless keeper . . .'

Other witnesses to the great event that day might well recall the scene somewhat differently. They might picture the boy's wild miskick in front of goal, then the ricochet off the post smacking him full in the face. The goalkeeper was indeed helpless – doubled up with laughter – and let the ball bobble its way into the net.

Luke's writing was nothing if not creative. Cocooned in his own virtual reality world of soccer dreams, he often reshaped history to match how he would have preferred things to be. He had already decided that he was going to be

a soccer reporter and commentator later in life – when he'd finally hung up his boots in the England dressing room for the last time.

For the moment, his notebook of footballing facts, figures and fiction gave him all the writing practice he needed, but what he wanted – what he really, really wanted – was extra practice at actually playing.

Luke closed the book with a sigh. 'The way things are going at school, I can't see the red pen being used much more,' he said to himself gloomily. 'And I don't suppose it'll get any better next season either . . .'

Luke went to lie on his bed and stare up at the football posters on the ceiling while he listened to the radio. Something the commentator was saying, however, suddenly made him pay extra attention.

'The player-manager has performed wonders. It's been a one-man show. He's taken the game by the scruff of the neck and given it a good shake, as if to say: "This is my team and I'll do what I like. I'm the boss!"'

'That's it!' exclaimed Luke, jumping off the bed in excitement. 'Why didn't I think of that before? Who cares if Frosty doesn't want me? I can form my own team to play in the Sunday League – and

pick myself to play centre-forward every week!'

He grabbed a sheet of file paper and began to write down some possible names for his new team.

Crawford Rangers, Luke's Legends, Luke's All Stars.

He wasn't satisfied. 'Perhaps it shouldn't really have my own name in it,' he mused. 'People might think it's being a bit big-headed.'

He tried out a few more, playing about with the names of macho-sounding animals, without coming to any decision.

The Rhinos, Swillsby Cougars, Swillsby Bulls.

Luke clattered downstairs. He knew he'd need the support of his parents if his idea was ever going to work. He doubted whether the League would let a twelve-year-old run a team all by himself.

'Don't you get enough football at school?' Dad said, knowing what a silly question it was as soon as he asked it.

Luke could never have enough football. As his soccer-mad son launched into his usual litany of complaints about Frosty's lack of encouragement, Dad realized he was fighting a losing battle. He decided the best policy was to humour him until even Luke saw that trying to start up a club would be too much of a thankless task.

'OK, OK, Luke, I get the message. Look, if you can persuade enough lads to join you, then I might consider it.'

'Great. Thanks, Dad. There's loads of lads like me who'd love to play Sunday football if there was a local side. Frosty puts them off with all his sarcastic remarks.'

'It doesn't seem to be working with you.'

Luke grinned. 'I only keep turning up 'cos I know it annoys him.'

Dad considered the list of names. 'Hmm.

Something with alliteration is usually best. More catchy.'

'What's that?' asked Luke.

'When the words start with the same sound, like . . . um . . .'

'Like *Swillsby Swifts*,' said Mum, coming into the room at that moment.

Luke liked the sound of that.

Next day, Luke went with Uncle Ray, Jon's dad, to watch his cousin play for Padley Panthers in a Sunday League cup game against Ashton Athletic.

Uncle Ray gave a little chuckle as he listened in the car to Luke's ambitious plans to form the Swifts. Then he made an offer that his nephew couldn't refuse. 'If you like, Luke, I could find a bit of space after Easter for an advert in the *Chronicle* to help you attract some players. It's about time Swillsby had a junior team again.'

Luke jumped at the chance of such publicity. Uncle Ray was the editor of the *Swillsby Chronicle*, the village's monthly free newspaper. It had to be free. Nobody would have bothered to buy it.

'Fantastic!' Luke enthused. 'I'll be able to sign up loads of stars. I'm on a scouting mission this

24

afternoon, in fact, talent-spotting.'

'Don't look at me like that,' Jon giggled at Luke's expectant face. 'I'm happy with the Panthers. We're gonna win the cup this season and Ashton sure aren't gonna stand in our way.'

'Why not?'

'Two reasons. Number one – they're in a lower league than us . . .'

'And number two?'

'Sanjay's playing in goal for them today!'

'I didn't know that,' Luke said, a little dismayed that his cousin knew something about football that he didn't. Luke could have invented his own version of *Trivial Pursuits* on the subject of football.

Jon shrugged. 'He's not their regular keeper, but I ain't surprised he stays pretty quiet about it. They're dead certs for relegation.'

The only reason Sanjay kept goal for the Comp was that Frosty couldn't persuade anybody else to play there. It wasn't that Sanjay was a bad keeper exactly. It was just that nobody quite knew what he would do next. He could go from hero to zero in less time than it took to slip the ball between his legs.

Jon's confident mood was in stark contrast to Sanjay's. The goalie grunted a greeting as Luke

strolled up behind the goal soon after the kick-off. 'Didn't expect to see you here.'

'Ditto,' said Luke. 'Thought you'd have had enough of Padley players for one weekend.'

'At least nobody's gonna give away hundreds of penalties this match.'

'It was only three,' Luke said indignantly.

Sanjay grinned. 'True. Must have been one of your better games.'

'I don't have the chance to have better games,' muttered Luke in response. 'Yesterday was my first – and probably my last.'

Sanjay was about to reply when he suddenly realized that the Panthers were heading his way, in alarming numbers. Through talking to Luke by the post, he was hopelessly out of position and Matthew's firm drive skimmed well out of his reach into the opposite corner.

'Goal!' Matthew cried. 'Thanks, Sanjay. Great start.'

Abuse rained down on Sanjay from his Ashton teammates. When he turned to vent his own fury on Luke, the post was deserted. Luke was already disappearing fast round the corner flag.

The goal was the first of many that afternoon. Matthew added another in the second half, Jon helped himself to a hat-trick and the rest of the

team made it a double-figures rout. Ashton's first-choice keeper was away sick, but it was doubtful whether he'd have fared any better than Sanjay. Even playing in goal together, they would have done well to keep the score down to less than half a dozen.

Luke congratulated his cousin after the final whistle. 'Great stuff, Johan. How many goals is that you've got this season?'

Jon gave his usual casual shrug. 'Dunno. Never keep count.'

Luke was gobsmacked. In Jon's shooting boots, he'd need new notebooks every month to have enough space for detailing his own goal-scoring feats.

He sidled up to Sanjay as the goalkeeper pulled off his boots outside the changing room. 'Bad luck, Sanjay. Could have been worse.'

Sanjay glared at him. 'Yeah, you could have been on the pitch.'

Luke ignored the cheap jibe. 'You'd be better off playing for some other team next season, I reckon,' he said. 'Y'know, one that fully appreciates your talents.'

'You trying to be funny?'

'No, I was just wondering. What if somebody came along and asked you to play for them

instead? Would you be interested?'

'All depends. Like who, for instance?'

'Me.'

Sanjay burst out laughing. '*You!* Come off it, you're just winding me up.'

'No, I'm dead serious. You see, I'm thinking of starting up a Sunday League team and I need a goalie.'

Sanjay sobered up. 'Listen, Luke. I wouldn't play in any team of yours if you paid me a million pounds. I'd have to be completely crazy. Read my lips. No way. Never. Not no how. Got it?'

He turned and stalked off inside, but Luke was not one to be deterred as easily as that.

'Think that means I can put him down as a possibility,' he murmured.

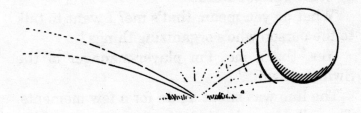

3 Wanted!

Early in the summer term a small display advert appeared on the sports page of the *Swillsby Chronicle*.

WANTED!
Under-13 Soccer Stars
For details, ring
Swillsby 433 424

It wasn't long before the phone rang and the receiver was snatched up.

'Hello, I want to speak to somebody about

the advert in the *Chronicle*.'

'That's me,' came the eager response.

There was a pause as a question mark of confusion slid down the line, eventually followed by some puzzled words.

'What do you mean, that's me? I want to talk to the person who's organizing things.'

'Yes, that's me. I'm player-manager of the Swillsby Swifts.'

The line was silent again for a few moments. The caller was clearly trying to work something out.

'I know that voice. It's Luke Crawford, isn't it?'

'Right first time. And I recognize you as well, Big Ben.'

'I don't believe this. *You* running a football team? Sanjay was laughing about it in the holidays, but I thought he was just joking.'

'No joke, Big Ben. I'm looking for players like you.'

'You're off your rocker!'

The phone went dead.

Luke sat by it in vain all evening, desperate for more enquiries. None came. He wondered whether Big Ben was somehow to blame.

After Sanjay's initial reaction, Luke hadn't yet plucked up the courage to approach any more of

his year group at the Comp. Ben Bradley was in the same class, a gawky, bespectacled youth who was already taller than some of the teachers. He was waiting for Luke next day outside their room – and so were a number of others.

'*Swillsby Swifts!*' Big Ben scoffed as Luke came round the corner of the corridor. 'What a stupid name!'

'More like the *Sloths!*' cackled Matthew. 'You'd have to be out of your tiny mind to want to play for Loony Luke!'

'Had any other phone calls?' sneered Sanjay.

'A couple actually, if you must know. Starting to put a useful squad together.'

They all burst out laughing. 'What rubbish!' Matthew taunted him. 'If you ever manage to form a team, I'll . . . I'll do a streak through assembly!'

They fell about at Matthew's threat, trying to imagine the look on the headmistress's face if he were ever to carry it out.

It was double Games for Year 7 that afternoon, an opportunity for Frosty to have everyone working up a sweat in the warm May sunshine. Luke was scampering around the running track, practising the 800 metres event when a figure in the discus area caught his eye.

It was difficult to miss Tubs. Almost as wide as he was high, Tubs swung his ample physique round and round, trying to copy muscular athletes he'd seen on TV. Suddenly the discus flew away, travelling a remarkable distance, but unfortunately in the wrong direction.

Luke and the other runners ducked in time, but Frosty had his back turned, bellowing at the backmarkers to get a move on. Something black and shiny whistled over his balding head and bounced across the track.

He whirled round to identify the culprit. 'What idiot threw that?' he barked.

Nobody had ever seen Tubs move quicker. He tried to melt into the queue waiting for their turn behind some netting, but it was like trying to hide a whale in a pack of fish fingers. Luke never heard what Frosty had to say, as he'd now rounded the far bend out of earshot, but he guessed the teacher wouldn't be asking Tubs to talk him through an action replay.

Luke chuckled to himself as he tried to stop Sanjay edging past him along the home straight. Like Big Ben, Tubs had played the odd game for the Comp in defence when Frosty had nobody else to turn to, but his wayward discus effort reminded Luke of Tubs's prodigious long throws.

'The Swifts could do with someone like that to take throw-ins,' Luke decided, crossing the line in third place ahead of Sanjay, much to the goalkeeper's disgust. 'I'll keep him in mind.'

As Luke arrived home, the phone went, but he didn't bother to answer it. Mum called him just as he opened the fridge for a cold drink.

'It's for you,' she said. 'Somebody called Brain or Drain, I think.'

If it had been anyone else, Luke might have indicated that he was out. He was expecting certain people to ring now, just to take the mickey, but Brain wasn't one of them. More importantly, Brain was a magic footballer.

'Hi, Brain,' he said cheerily. 'What d'yer want?'

'Er, I'm ringing about that advert of yours,' came the hesitant reply.

Luke doubted whether Brain would have read it. Reading wasn't exactly his strongpoint. Nor was spelling. That's why *Brian* usually came out as *Brain*, and the nickname had stuck.

'What about it? Everybody seems to think it's a huge joke.'

'Well, I don't. If you're gonna start a new team, count me in, OK?'

Luke's hand was still trembling as he put down the phone. He'd got his first recruit for the

Swifts – Brian Draper. And with someone like him on board, Luke was hopeful that others would soon follow. The only reason Brain didn't play for the Comp was that he was scared of Frosty.

'But he's *good*,' said Big Ben in amazement the following day when Luke proudly broke the news to him at lunchtime. 'In fact, he's brilliant. What's Brain doing getting mixed up with the Swifts?'

' 'Cos we're going places,' Luke beamed. 'He's got the sense to want to be in on it right from the start.'

'Listen, Luke,' said Big Ben, checking that nobody else was nearby. 'Sorry if I went a bit over the top about the Swifts. I reckon it's a good idea of yours really, but I was just caught by surprise, you know.'

Luke affected a shrug. 'Already forgotten about,' he lied.

'Yeah, well, I might still be interested in playing, especially with Brain in the team. But just keep it to yourself for now, right? If you blab, I'll kill you.'

Luke nodded. 'No problem. It's our secret, OK, trust me.'

Big Ben gave him another warning look, the

light glinting menacingly off his specs, then wandered off. Luke could have hugged himself.

'That's three,' he said under his breath. 'Only eight more to go and we can make up a team. Watch out, Matthew, we'll have you streaking across that hall yet!'

He spotted Sanjay sauntering towards the dining room and moved off to intercept. 'Hey, Sanjay!' he called out. 'You got a minute?'

Luke sat next to the goalkeeper in the hall to eat their packed lunches and Tubs came to join them. Tubs helped himself to some of theirs too, besides tucking into his own.

'Well, what was it you wanted to ask me that was so important?' said Sanjay, stuffing his mouth full of crisps.

Luke glanced at Tubs. He'd rather have tackled each one separately but now the chance had presented itself, he decided he might as well go for it.

'I'd like you and Tubs to come and play for the Swifts!'

Sanjay shared his crisps with Tubs too, spluttering them out across the table as Tubs's deep belly laugh rumbled around the hall.

'Any team that might want *me* in their side can't be worth playing for,' Tubs guffawed.

'It must be rubbish.'

'Not with Brain on the wing, it won't be.'

'Brain!' exclaimed Sanjay, shocked. 'No kidding?'

'Who else you got?' asked Tubs out of curiosity.

Luke was on delicate ground on this subject, but knew he couldn't pull back now and just say nobody. Negotiations were at a crucial stage. He had to keep making things sound impressive.

'Look, I can only tell you this in strict confidence, right?' he began.

'OK, OK, spare us all the hype,' snapped Sanjay. 'Spit it out.'

'All right, but one word out of place and I'm dead.'

'Don't tempt us,' grinned Tubs.

Luke lowered his voice. 'Big Ben's agreed to join too.'

'Big Ben! Is that all?' sneered Sanjay. 'No other big names?'

'There's Andrzej Leszczyszak, that Polish kid,' suggested Tubs. 'Names don't come much bigger than his in Year Seven!'

'I'm trying to build the spine of the team first,' Luke told them, attempting a spot of flattery. 'That's the real strength of a side, down the middle. With you in goal, Sanjay, Tubs and Big Ben as centre-backs, plus me at centre-forward . . .'

Tubs grinned. 'Sounds like it's got about as much spine as a jellyfish.'

'I'd have thought that Tubs would be more like the extra flesh on the bones,' put in Sanjay, seizing the chance of a jibe at his pal's expense.

Luke felt in danger of losing credibility in the face of their continued jests. 'And my cousin is also thinking of seeking a transfer . . .' he said in desperation.

 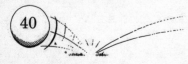

'Jon leaving the Panthers?' gasped Sanjay. 'Cool, man! Now you're really talking.'

Luke crossed his fingers under the table. Anything was possible, he reasoned. He hadn't actually said that Jon was joining the Swifts. Just hinted, that's all. No harm in that, was there?

'I could guarantee both you guys a game every week,' he promised, holding out more bait. 'How about that?'

'I'll have to think about it,' said Tubs, standing up and brushing all the crumbs off his bulging jumper on to the floor. 'I'll let you know.'

'So, what about you, Sanjay?'

'Might do. Where are we gonna play?'

Luke didn't have an answer for that yet, but he still took heart from the question. It was the first time that anybody had said *we*.

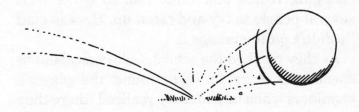

4 Aye, Aye, Skipper!

Luke's recruitment drive during the summer term met with limited success. He even went to watch a seven-a-side tournament at the primary school one Saturday to see if there was any talent on view.

He was on the point of leaving, disappointed, when a wonderful piece of skill caught his eye. A slim, dark-haired player dribbled through the opposition defence with amazing ball control before curling a shot into the bottom left-hand corner of the small goal.

'Magic!' breathed Luke. 'Wonder if he plays for any Sunday side yet?'

Ever optimistic, the Swifts' self-appointed chief scout intended to find out. After the game, the number four scuttled away towards the changing rooms and Luke had to barge past several people to try and catch up. He was glad he didn't quite manage it.

As they reached the school, Luke was about to speak and wrap his arm round the player's shoulders when he suddenly realized where they were heading. He veered off just in time. Red-faced, he sidled across the playing field, homewards, hoping that nobody had noticed how he'd nearly followed the number four into the girls' toilet.

'Pity!' he muttered, cursing his luck and the rules against mixed teams. 'She was a good little footballer too.'

On the Comp's Sports Day in June, Luke was watching the sprint races with keen interest, looking for someone who might inject a bit of extra pace into the Swifts' attack. He particularly wanted to see David Richards in action, a lad he'd spotted in Games bombing up the track in training for the 100 metres event. Dazza was new to the school this term and Luke wondered what he was like with a ball at his feet.

As the gun sounded for Dazza's heat, Luke

44

was grabbed from behind and wrestled to the ground. He had no chance to escape. Pinned down by two heavier bodies, he squinted up into the sun to see the leering faces of Big Ben and Matthew. Somebody, he realized immediately, had dropped him in it.

'Well, well, look what we've got here – a poacher!' sneered Matthew.

'A po . . . poacher?' stammered Luke, trying to collect his wits.

'Yeah, and a blabbermouth,' hissed Big Ben.

Luke wasn't in much of a position to shrug. Matthew was kneeling on his chest. 'Soz, Big Ben, I just thought that if people knew you were going to be their teammate, they might be more willing to join as well.'

Big Ben was in no mood for any flannel and pressed down harder on Luke's legs. 'Well, you've lost me now 'cos of that. You'll have to go and find yourself a new centre-back.'

'Poaching other teams' players ain't allowed,' Matthew stated. 'No way is Jon or anybody else leaving the Panthers. Understand?'

'Sure, Matt. I wasn't . . .'

'Shut it! This is just a gentle warning, Loony Luke. If I hear you're tapping any of our players, you know what to expect, right?'

'Right,' Luke gurgled as Matthew accidentally on purpose leant on his throat as he heaved himself up and swaggered away with Big Ben.

Luke was left spreadeagled on the grass, pretending to be sunbathing. 'Just a temporary setback, that's all,' he murmured to himself. 'Bound to be a few hiccups in the transfer market from time to time . . .'

Luke arranged a training session for the would-be Swifts in the first week of the summer holidays.

'What time are the others coming?' asked Dazza, pulling off his shirt to enjoy the feel of the sun on his back.

Tubs wished he could do the same, but was conscious that his rippling rolls of fat wouldn't bear public comparison with Dazza's rippling muscles. 'What others?' he chuckled. 'I reckon we're all here.'

'But Luke told me this was a team practice.'

Sanjay cut in. 'He must have meant a five-a-side team!'

They gazed across to where Luke was exchanging short passes with Brain outside the recreation ground's changing cabin. At least that

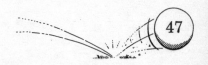

was the idea. Luke's passes were mostly sprayed into the woodwork behind Brain and he collected the rebounds.

Luke was in full football kit, his orange shirt – Holland's colours – bearing the number nine. It was his favourite number, even though he'd have liked one with Johan Cruyff's famous 14 on it too.

'Hey, Luke!' called Sanjay. 'Is this it? Five players?'

Luke took his eye off the ball and missed it completely, leaving it for Brain to fetch. 'Well, there would have been a couple more, but they're on holiday this week . . .' he said and carried on speaking before anyone could ask who the missing people were '. . . and there's Big Ben as well . . .'

'I thought . . .'

'He's just playing hard to get, that's all. He'll turn up one day as soon as he stops sulking, you'll see. Anyway, let's get cracking, men.'

'Too hot to go charging about today,' grumbled Tubs.

'We'll only have a gentle jog round the recky to start with,' said Luke. 'Follow your skipper, everybody.'

They watched him tear off towards the trees.

'Just look at that boy go,' grinned Dazza.

'That's all I'm gonna do, just look,' said Tubs, slumping down on to the grass. 'If he expects me to run, I'm going home.'

It took Luke a little while to realize his teammates were somewhat slow off the mark. He wandered back to them sheepishly.

'Er, you were supposed to come after me. I was just setting the pace.'

'I was impressed,' said Dazza, his grin ever wider. 'Surprised you didn't win your race on Sports Day.'

Luke glanced at Sanjay and pulled a face. 'Might have done if somebody hadn't gone and tripped me up on the first bend.'

Sanjay was a picture of innocence. 'We were all too bunched up after the gun. Could have been anybody.'

'C'mon, Luke, let's just play footie today,' said Brain, juggling a ball on his knees and trainers. 'We'll get enough exercise doing that.'

Luke reluctantly agreed. 'OK, but I would like to mention one thing, men. It's Skipper, not Luke, when we're together as Swifts, right?'

Tubs found it impossible to keep a straight face, especially when his was so round with multiple chins. 'Aye, aye, Skipper! Anything you say, Skipper,' he chuckled. 'Apart from making me run, of course.'

They began a game of two against two. Luke and Brain paired up to play Tubs and Dazza, with Sanjay acting as the neutral keeper in a makeshift goal of shirts and water bottles. He was wearing one of his garishly patterned tops, always wanting to look the part of a proper goal-keeper.

Appearances can be deceptive. Brain's first shot skimmed right between his legs into the goal.

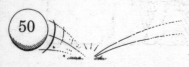

'One–nil!' cried Luke. 'I'll keep the score.'

Sanjay hoofed the ball away for Luke and Dazza to give chase, but there was only ever going to be one winner, despite Luke's head start. Dazza swooped on to the ball, then tripped and lost control as he went too fast for his own limited ball skills. Luke gleefully took over possession.

As Tubs lumbered towards him, blocking his path to goal like a ten-ton truck on a country lane, Luke attempted to chip the ball over his head. He connected well, but failed to get the intended height or direction. The ball flew into Tubs's bobbling midriff, rearranging his breakfast.

Play was halted while Tubs discovered how to breathe again.

'Soz, Tubs,' Luke apologized. 'I was just trying to find Brain.'

'Well, he ain't in there, Luke,' he wheezed, rubbing his stomach.

Luke considered reminding him about being called Skipper, but decided that wouldn't perhaps be appreciated just at this moment.

'What we need are some real opponents so we can all play together on the same side,' he said.

'What, all five of us?' said Sanjay sarcastically.

'What about the Scouts?' Brain piped up. 'Bet they could give us a game.'

'Hey, wicked idea, Brain!' Luke enthused. 'Yeah, Swillsby Scouts. Any of you lot in the Scouts?'

They shook their heads. 'I know someone who is,' said Brain. 'Mark Stringer. He lives next door to me. I'll ask him, OK?'

'We'd be better off playing the Brownies!' Sanjay muttered as he trudged back into goal. He just wished that Ashton hadn't given him the sack.

Their mistake-ridden kickabout spluttered on for another twenty minutes until they finally became aware of a spectator, leaning against the cabin.

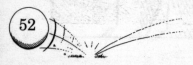

'Hi, Titch,' Tubs greeted him. 'Didn't see you there.'

'He's a bit harder to spot than you, even when he's standing up,' Sanjay grinned.

'I *am* standing up,' Titch retorted, well used to Sanjay's strange sense of humour. 'Can I play?'

'Don't know. Can you?' panted Luke, his thin face red and blotchy from all his exertions. 'Not seen you play footie before.'

'Never too late to start, is it?'

'Same with growing,' put in Sanjay.

Titch ignored him. 'So what do I have to do to get a game, Luke?'

'Just call him Skipper,' grinned Tubs. 'That'll make him happy.'

'All right, I suppose we could give you a trial,' Luke conceded, trying to sound superior. 'See if you might be good enough for the Swifts.'

Titch looked around idly. 'The rest on holiday, are they?' he said.

'Touchy point, that. I shouldn't ask, if I were you,' Sanjay smirked.

He might have been small, but Titch soon showed Luke how hard he could tackle. Going for a fifty-fifty ball, Titch surprised him with the force of his challenge and Luke finished up on his backside. He then slid a pass through to Dazza who drove the ball under Sanjay's dive for

another goal. Even Luke had lost track of the score by now.

'Is that good enough for you . . . Skipper?' said Titch with a smile.

Luke was still sitting down and seemed to have come to a decision on the spot. 'Er, yeah, how would you like to join the Swifts, Titch? I reckon we could do with a tiger tackler like you in midfield.'

'Tell Mark to make that a six-a-side match now, Brain,' said Tubs. 'Or better still, don't. They may not notice we've got an extra man.'

'Yeah – especially if it's Titch!' said Sanjay.

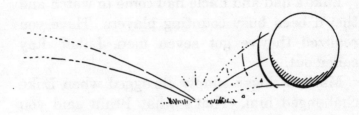

5   Talent Scouts

The hastily arranged game against the Scouts took place early the following week. It was played on a small pitch behind the scout hut, in a field normally used for grazing cattle. Fresh evidence of their occupation was all too clear to see – and smell.

Big Ben gave Luke a smirk before the kick-off. He was keen to make his mark in the match, preferably on the legs of the Swifts' skipper.

'Didn't know you were in the Scouts,' Luke said to him.

'No secret – just like something else I could mention,' Big Ben replied, still smirking. 'You lot are gonna get stuffed tonight.'

'Don't count your chickens. We've been practising.'

Luke's dad and uncle had come to watch and they'd been busy counting players. 'Have you realized they've got seven men, Luke?' Ray called out.

Mark Stringer simply shrugged when Luke challenged him. 'That's what Brain said you wanted, seven-a-side, so that's how many we picked.'

'Well, Brain got it wrong. We only have six players altogether.'

'Tough. We can't help it if you turn up a man short.'

'He must be talking about you, Titch!' smirked Sanjay, never able to resist a size-ist joke.

'Haven't you got somebody spare we can borrow?' said Luke.

Mark sighed and looked round at some of the other scouts nearby. 'Sean, you fancy a game?'

Luke recognized Sean from school, but had barely ever spoken to him. His uniform looked immaculate, with badges all the way along his sleeves.

'Might do,' Sean said casually. 'As long as our kit's clean.'

'You'll be playing for them.'

Sean gazed with obvious distaste at the hotch-potch of gear that the Swifts were wearing. Uncle Ray had managed to scrounge an old, discarded outfit from the Panthers that looked as if it had been through the wash too many times. But not recently. The shirts were now a faded, smudgy yellow and the shorts could best be described as off-white. Only Luke and Sanjay could boast clean, bright strips of their own.

'Do I have to?' Sean whined.

'Yes, you do,' Mark ordered. 'And get a move on.'

The twenty-minute first period was half over before Sean emerged from the hut. He'd spent the last few minutes examining his appearance in a mirror. The score was still level, amazingly, at 1–1, with Sanjay grateful to be playing in small goals. Shots had whistled high and wide out of his reach, which in full-sized goals might well have gone in.

Brain had scored for the Swifts, pleased to make up for his mistake over the numbers. He'd cancelled out the Scouts' opening goal by slipping the ball through Big Ben's long legs and then steering it home from a narrow angle past the motionless keeper.

Sean's first touch, sadly, went the wrong way. It put the Swifts in trouble, with Tubs caught out of position in defence, but it allowed Sanjay to enjoy his finest moment. He covered himself in glory for once with a spectacular save, diving to his left to cling on to a fizzing shot.

Unfortunately, it wasn't all he was covered in. As Sanjay stood up, ball safely in his grasp, he looked down the side of his kit in disgust and swore loudly.

'Pooh, Sanjay!' exclaimed Tubs, wrinkling his nose. 'Never mind, at least it should make their attackers keep their distance from you. Nobody will want to be close enough to snap up anything you drop!'

'Sorry, guys,' Sean apologized. 'Got a bit confused there. Forgot I wasn't playing for the Scouts.'

To his credit, Sean did try his best for the Swifts. His style of play was as neat and stylish as he liked to dress, passing the ball short and usually accurately. He was also left-footed.

Luke's running commentary was thinking ahead. *Sean would give the Swifts a better balance with that sweet left foot of his. He links up with the skipper now and Luke Crawford's*

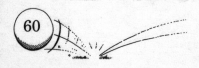

clear . . . Ugghhh! The skipper's down, fouled by Big Ben, but the ref's waved play-on. He must be blind . . .'

Luke had been racing up and down the pitch like an overwound clockwork toy, desperate for his team to do well and impress his dad. The fate of the Swifts might depend upon this performance. Dad hadn't yet agreed to register the Swifts in the Sunday League for the new season and time was running out. This match could be make or break.

Perhaps Luke was trying too hard. He charged back to regain possession and went for the ball at the same time as Titch. Their collision left the striker free to shoot and he lashed the ball past the groping Sanjay.

'Thanks a bunch,' said Titch sarcastically. 'Just what I needed, that, a kick on the shin from my own skipper.'

The Swifts were 2–1 down at half-time and Luke put on his player-manager's hat to give the team a pep-talk. 'We've got to test their keeper out more, men. He's definitely dodgy. Shoot every chance you get and one's bound to go in. There's no reason why we can't go on to win this . . .'

'I can give you one,' Sanjay interrupted. 'We're rubbish!'

Luke talked for the whole of the break, rambling on about what he wanted each player to do in the second period. His team weren't really listening. The juicy orange slices commanded more of their attention.

Luke's plans overlooked one thing – his own knack of putting his foot in it. Or his head. Soon after the restart, the skipper glanced a Scouts' corner perfectly off the back of his head into the gap between Sanjay and the far post. He couldn't have placed it better if he'd tried. In fact, if he had tried to do it, he'd never even have got it close.

'Brilliant!' snarled Sanjay. 'How does that boy do it?'

Luke had no answer to that and his commentary didn't attempt to explain it either. *'After that unlucky deflection the Swifts will have to battle even harder now, but you can be sure of one thing. Skipper Luke Crawford will not allow his men to accept defeat without a fight . . .'*

It looked an uphill task. Mark and Big Ben had been doing a good steady job together in defence for the Scouts. Dazza's pace sometimes troubled them, if not his ball control, but their main worry was Brain. The only way to get the ball off the winger, it seemed, was to foul him.

Finally, they paid the price. After Mark bundled him over, Brain promptly drilled the free-kick into the bottom corner to reduce the lead. And when he jinked his way goalwards again, weaving between the cowpats along the touchline, the two big defenders had to be doubly careful.

Brain drew them both towards him like moths to a candle flame before knocking the ball across to the unmarked Dazza to set up the equalizer. Dazza's close-range shot wouldn't have gone in, however, without some help from the keeper. The boy half-stopped it, but could only fumble

the ball over the line. He thumped the ground in annoyance and then wished he hadn't done that. There was a sickly squelch and the muck splattered up from his fist into his face.

At 3–3, the match was on a knife-edge and the honour of scoring a late winning goal fell to a Scout. Ironically, it was Sean.

The Swifts' loan player had sauntered up the left wing behind Brain, not expecting to receive the ball, when Brain suddenly screwed it back to him. Sean didn't have time to think. He simply swung his left foot and the ball flew into the net an instant before he was buried beneath a mob of laughing teammates. He wasn't quite so popular with his fellow Scouts.

It proved a profitable evening all round for Luke. Besides the morale-boosting 4–3 victory, he made a potential gain of three more players. Both Mark and Sean expressed an interest in joining the Swifts and he made peace again with Big Ben.

'Forgive and forget?' Luke offered as they shook hands after the game. 'I'd still like to have you in the team. What d'yer say, eh?'

Big Ben nodded. 'Well, I'd love to play Sunday football, but nobody else seems to want a short-sighted, lumbering giraffe in their defence.'

'Can't think why, can you?' Luke said and they grinned at each other.

But most important of all was Dad's favourable reaction to what he'd seen. 'Reckon you deserve to be given a chance, Luke,' he said. 'The boys really tried hard tonight. Shows the team must mean something to them.'

Uncle Ray agreed. 'I'm willing to help out too, at least with filling in all the forms and that. I know the League Secretary. I'll get in touch with him tomorrow and make sure he finds us a place in the League.'

As soon as they returned home, Luke raced upstairs to his bedroom and took a brand new notebook out of his desk. He had bought it at the weekend to celebrate this grand occasion – the birth of the Swifts!

He carefully began to log the details of their first win in red ink. As skipper, coach and player-manager, he'd make sure all the future entries in this book were written in red too. He was now the Boss!

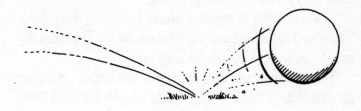

6 Friendly Farce

'I've fixed up a pre-season friendly for us,' Luke announced at one of the Swifts' regular training sessions. 'Eleven-a-side.'

'Have we actually got eleven players?' asked Tubs. 'The most we've ever had for a practice so far is nine.'

'That's only because of holidays and suchlike,' said Luke, dismissing the query out of hand. 'Make sure you'll all be free to play on Tuesday, men. Six o'clock kick-off here on the recky, OK?'

Brain looked doubtful. 'Next Tuesday? Think I've got something else on then, Skipper.'

'Well, cancel it. What's more important than playing for the Swifts?'

Sean answered for him. 'If you've got a couple of hours, I'll make you a list,' he said cheekily. 'Anyway, who are we playing?'

'It's against a team called Desdale Rangers. They're just starting up like us so we'll probably meet them again in the league.'

'You mean in the bottom division,' Sanjay grumbled. 'That's where your uncle said we'll be dumped.'

'We can't expect to go straight into the premier league, can we?' said Luke. 'We'll have to work our way up, getting promoted each season.'

'Fat chance of that!' scoffed Big Ben.

Before Luke could chivvy his players into action, Ray turned up with his camera.

'Bit early, ain't it, Skip, for a team photo?' said Dazza. 'With Titch away, there's only eight of us here.'

'Seven,' Mark corrected him. 'As soon as he spotted the camera, Sean nipped off to fetch his comb!'

'It's individual mugshots I want today,' Ray explained. 'We've got to have your ugly faces on the registration forms, in case anybody wants to check your identity.'

'That's so we can't play Jon in a match, for example, and pretend he's Tubs,' grinned Luke.

Tubs looked aggrieved, knowing it would pave the way for another cheap jibe by Sanjay. The goalkeeper didn't miss the chance.

'Ye-es, I see,' he drawled. 'That's a good idea. It's easy to get the two of them mixed up. I do it all the time!'

Fifteen minutes of hilarity followed as each player posed against the side wall of the changing cabin while the others pulled faces at him behind Ray's back. Then they did it all over again after he remembered to put some film into his camera.

'Sorry about that, lads,' Ray apologized. 'Oh, and there are a couple of other matters to sort out as well soon. One: we'll need a copy of your birth certificate to prove your age . . .'

'Everybody knows the skipper's birthday,' laughed Big Ben.

Luke reddened. 'Not my fault if I was born on the first of April!'

'. . . and two: we've got to decide how much your match fee should be.'

'Hey, wicked!' cried Dazza. 'I didn't know we got paid to play.'

Sanjay put a hand on his shoulder in mock comfort. 'Er, I'm afraid it doesn't quite work like that, Dazza,' he sniggered. 'We have to pay them, not the other way round.'

'What! You never said anything about this, Skip,' Dazza protested.

'Didn't I?' Luke said innocently. 'Soz, must have slipped my mind. It's an expensive business, running a team, you know. All sorts of costs

to meet – pitch hire, washing the kit, buying foot-balls, you name it.'

'Might not have agreed to sign up, if I'd known,' Dazza muttered.

'That's why he kept quiet about it,' Tubs chuckled. 'Not always as daft as he looks, our skipper.'

At last the practice began. His dad and uncle were more than happy to leave all the training to Luke, and the players didn't mind him being in charge unless he tried to get too bossy – or expected them to do too much running about. More energetic fitness work, Luke realized, would have to wait till cooler weather.

During a break in a four-a-side kickabout, Brain suddenly remembered why Tuesday rang a bell with him. 'Soz, Skipper, I won't be able to play in that friendly. It's my birthday.'

'Can't you have your birthday another day?'

Brain shook his head. 'Like you said, I can't help the day I was born. Got a big family do at a posh restaurant. It's all booked and that.'

Luke threw up his hands in despair. 'OK, OK, we'll just have to manage without you somehow, I suppose,' he said grudgingly. 'But listen, men, rule number one – keep Sundays clear once the season starts. No excuses. Trips out and birthday parties are banned, right?'

There were a few grunts and nods in response.

'Power's gone to his head,' hissed Sanjay, nudging Tubs. 'He'll have that rule written into the league handbook, given half a chance.'

Tuesday evening was a disaster from start to finish. In fact, things went wrong even before the match. The teams arrived to find the cabin locked up with the goal nets inside, the pitch not yet marked out and the lines from last season almost invisible in the long grass.

The Swifts again had to beg for the loan of players. They only had nine men – including Brain. He'd insisted on playing first before going out for the meal, but his reward for such loyalty was a clout in the mouth during the game that made eating later a painful experience.

And to make matters even worse, it was raining. It began in the first half when the Swifts were already losing 3–0 and a cloudburst midway through the second mercifully put an end to the farce. The match was abandoned with the score about 8–0, but hardly anyone cared enough to keep a count by then. With nowhere to shelter, players and spectators alike were drenched to the skin.

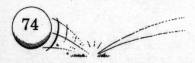

People often say that every cloud has a silver lining. They're wrong. These were simply dirty, big, black ones full of rain.

'That was just about the most miserable night of my life,' groaned Dad the following evening. 'If that's a taste of what running a football team can be like, then forget it. It's not worth it.'

'C'mon, Dad. It wasn't as bad as all that,' Luke replied anxiously. 'Bound to be a few teething problems.'

'Think I'd rather have all my teeth pulled out without painkillers than go through that again.'

'Can we leave the subject of teeth, please?' said Mum. 'I've got an appointment at the dentist's tomorrow.'

'Soz, Mum. So has poor old Brain.'

'Bet he's got water on the brain now as well,' said Dad with a grimace.

Luke smirked. 'That's easy to cure. He just needs a tap on the head!'

It was an old joke and Dad had temporarily lost his sense of humour. 'Name me one thing, Luke, that was good about last night.'

'Umm . . .'

'Exactly. We all got soaked for nothing. I've a good mind to cancel our application to join the League . . .'

'Too late. We're already in!' Uncle Ray's arrival could not have been better timed. He flourished a small book under his brother's nose. 'Just received this, the official handbook with all the fixtures in it.'

'Fantastic!' cried Luke in relief. He was dying to see their name in print, confirming the existence of the Swifts beyond any doubt. 'Who have we got first?'

Ray grinned and passed him the book. 'Take a look for yourself, Skipper. It's your team.'

Luke scrabbled through the pages until he found the opening fixtures and then gazed at the list for several moments, as if in disbelief. There the Swifts were, in black and white. His dream had turned into reality.

'We're away – against Fenthorpe Forest,' he croaked at last. 'Are they any good?'

'No idea, but I guess we'll soon find out,' said his uncle before making Luke a stunning offer. 'To mark the Big Kick-Off, how would you like to write a short match report of the Forest game for the *Chronicle*? I'm sure we could find a bit of space for it on the sports page.'

Luke was speechless, but the wide-eyed look on his face said it all. He was in soccer paradise. His very own match report. In the *Chronicle*. To be read by everyone in the village . . .

He was not only a player-manager now, but a football journalist too!

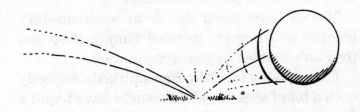

7   The Big Kick-Off

By the time of the Swifts' final practice session before making their League debut, Luke had somehow scraped together exactly eleven players.

'Do you want any help in choosing the team for Sunday, Skipper?' asked Sanjay mischievously.

Luke gave him a look. He'd expected his goal-keeper to make some sort of facetious remark like that. 'No thanks,' he replied curtly. 'I think I can manage. We'll just have to hope we don't need any subs.'

'Skip's banning all injuries as well as

birthdays,' announced Dazza.

Luke sighed as the rest laughed. 'Would have been all right if I hadn't been let down by a few people. They promised to sign for the Swifts and then went off to join other teams.'

'You've been going on about such mystery players all summer,' grinned Sanjay. 'I reckon they only existed in your imagination.'

'C'mon, fair's fair,' Big Ben smirked. 'Anybody with a bit of sense or ability would have found a decent team to play for instead.'

'*We're* a decent team,' Luke insisted. 'Or at least we will be once I've knocked you all into shape.'

Tubs let loose his rumbling laugh. 'You'll have to get a big hammer. The only shape I'm ever gonna be is round!'

'The way I see it,' said Titch, 'is that it's a good job there is no competition for places, otherwise half of us wouldn't get a look in.'

Tubs nodded. 'Face facts, Skipper. Nobody else wants us. We're the dregs at the bottom of soccer's cup!'

'Rubbish!' retorted Luke. 'I don't want the dregs either. You're all here for positive reasons.'

'Hello, this should make interesting listening,' said Sanjay. 'C'mon, then, Skipper, spill the

beans. What are these hidden talents each of us have that make us so special?'

Luke was put on the spot. 'Well . . .' he began uncertainly, 'I mean, every team needs different sorts of players, you know, with their own strengths. No good being all the same – unless you had eleven Johan Cruyffs of course. You want people who are best at marking and tackling, people with stamina who graft in midfield, people with speed who can dribble the ball . . .'

'Er, you haven't mentioned goalies yet,' interrupted Sanjay. 'People who can keep the ball out of your own net. They're quite important.'

'Right, I was just coming to that. You see, that's why you've all been picked to play for the Swifts – to do these various jobs in the side.'

'I'm still not sure where I come in,' chuckled Tubs. 'I don't seem to fit into any of them categories.'

'Well, you've got a long throw and a good hard kick . . .'

Sanjay cut in again. 'And we can always use you to flatten out the molehills on the pitch!'

Brain turned up at that moment, late as usual, just as Tubs was threatening to flatten Sanjay instead.

'And here's the guy who's gonna score a lot

of our goals,' added Luke.

'Soz, Skipper. I got the time a bit mixed up. Who are they?'

Brain was looking over to where two track-suited lads were warming up near the cabin, going through a sequence of stretching exercises.

'Craig and Jordan, apparently,' said Sean. 'They've only just moved into the village. They don't know the skipper yet so that's why he's been able to fool them into joining the Swifts.'

'Right couple of dummies by the look of them,' muttered Sanjay. 'You wait till you see them trying to play football. It's hilarious.'

'So what are *their* secret qualities, Skipper?' asked Mark.

Luke seemed evasive, but Mark was as persistent as a dogged defender should be. 'C'mon, tell us the real reasons. If we've all got our uses, what are theirs?'

'Well, OK, Craig's parents have got a big car. It'll come in handy for transport to away matches.'

'Might have guessed there'd be some motive to your madness,' cackled Sanjay. 'And Jordan? Has his mum promised to bake some cakes for half-time refreshments?'

'Don't be stupid,' snapped Luke, then shrugged. 'Oh, well, if you must know. I was hoping to keep it a surprise. He says his dad knows somebody who can get us a team strip, dead cheap, like . . .'

The players broke away, laughing among themselves.

'Huh! Let them mock,' Luke murmured. 'They won't mind when I give out a brand new kit for them to wear. It'll be "Good old Jordan" then, I bet, and not a word of thanks to me.'

The others soon saw what Sanjay meant about their new recruits. Craig seemed to have two left feet, neither of which knew how to kick a ball,

and Jordan simply had no idea about the game. He tackled anybody within range, no matter which side they were on, and toe-ended the ball in the direction that he happened to be facing. He reminded them a little of Luke.

It was no great surprise, therefore, when Jordan failed to turn up at the arranged meeting place for the short journey to Fenthorpe. They waited for him as long as possible, but finally had to leave without him. They also left without Craig's car. It had broken down.

'Looks like it's the pukey yellow kit again, guys,' sighed Sean.

That was Luke's biggest disappointment. Not so much that Jordan's absence meant they only had ten players, but the fact that he'd set his heart on the Swifts parading their new team strip. Jordan had assured him his dad would produce it today before the match.

'What a start!' Luke muttered under his breath in the back of his dad's battered old van. 'Things can only get better from now on, surely.'

That just shows how wrong you can be.

'Right, men. All ready?' cried Luke in the visitors' changing room.

There was no response. 'I said "All ready?"'

he repeated. 'Remember what I wanted you all to shout back?'

They looked at him blankly. 'You mean that wasn't a joke?' said Sanjay. 'You really expect us to perform that charade?'

'It's not a charade,' Luke told him. 'It's all to do with team spirit, bonding together before a match. Going out there to face the enemy all fired up, willing to die for each other.'

'Steady on, Skip,' grinned Dazza. 'It's only a footie match.'

'C'mon, men, let's try it again. You'll get to enjoy it.'

'Ready, Skipper,' Brain called out. His was a lone voice and he felt a little foolish.

'Not yet, Brain. I haven't said my bit yet,' smiled Luke.

'Well, come on, then, let's get it over with, or it'll be half-time before we get out on the pitch,' grumbled Big Ben.

Luke took a deep breath. 'Right, men. All ready?'

There was a muted, embarrassed chorus. 'Ready, Skipper.'

'I can see that's something else we'll have to practise,' Luke sighed. 'OK, let's go. Let the Swifts fly free!'

'Hold on a sec, Skipper, I'm not ready.'

It was Tubs. He was still trying to squeeze a tight yellow shirt over his head and his vest. 'Somebody else must have pinched the shirt I had in that friendly,' he complained. 'This one doesn't fit me.'

'Perhaps it shrunk in all that rain,' suggested Dazza.

'You'll have to shrink a bit, too,' grinned Sanjay. 'And better make sure your shorts don't split as well. We don't want the game abandoned 'cos of an exploding Tubs!'

Luke sat down on a bench, head in his hands. When Tubs was finally sorted out, the skipper couldn't be bothered to go through the whole routine again. He just opened the door of the changing room and led his ten men outside. There would be no borrowing a player for this match. League points were at stake.

Luke's plan to play 4–2–4 had to be readjusted into a loose – very loose – 4–2–1–2 line up. *Flexible* was the term he used to describe it, but nobody understood what the skipper meant when he said that he himself was going to be the '1', playing in the hole behind the two main strikers.

'Playing "in the hole"?' asked Titch as they

lined up, watching where he put his feet. 'What's he going on about?'

'Dunno,' admitted Brain with a shrug. 'But if you suddenly disappear from view, I guess we'll know that you've found it!'

Luke had the honour of kicking off the Swifts' first season, but he wasn't so thrilled to have to do it three more times inside the opening ten minutes. He was soon wishing there was a real hole that he might have been able to hide himself in.

The Swifts were swamped. There seemed to be twice as many red shirts on the field as their own yellows, not just an extra one. Luke watched the fourth goal go in with a sense of doom, the kind when you know something awful is going to happen, but can't do anything to stop it. He simply let his commentary describe the inevitable outcome.

'. . . A Forest striker latches on to the pass, unchallenged, and can hardly believe his luck. Where's the marking? It's all up to Sanjay now. The Swifts' keeper is quick off his line to narrow the angle and the shot's hit straight at him. He blocks it, but the ball runs loose and the number eight has just tapped it into the empty net. Oh, Sanjay! Oh, Swifts! This is a disaster . . .'

88

By half-time, it was seven.

'So how do we get out of this mess?' asked Titch.

'We do a rain dance,' said Tubs. 'See if we can start up another storm to get this match washed out as well.'

No such luck. The August sky was a clear, cloudless blue. If there was a god of football somewhere up there, he obviously didn't support the Swifts.

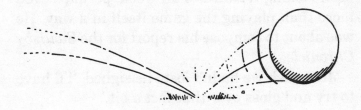

8   Goalhanger

After tea, Luke sat in front of the computer in his bedroom with mixed emotions. He was upset that the Swifts had lost their first league match so heavily, but relieved that his players seemed to have taken the defeat quite well, all things considered.

They'd just laughed it off. No-one had blamed the manager, nor the coach, nor even the skipper. He was grateful for that at least, since he would have been the target of abuse in each case.

'Team spirit must be good,' he mused. 'Gives

us something to build on, I suppose.'

Despite his own personal disappointment, Luke was also excited. He opened a new file on the word processor. This was the moment he'd been looking forward to all week, perhaps even more than playing the game itself in a way. He was about to compose his report for the *Swillsby Chronicle*.

'Just wish we hadn't lost,' he sighed. 'I'll have to try and gloss over that fact a bit.'

With the final score being 13–0, that was not going to be an easy task. Luke scribbled a few notes down on some scrap paper and then began to tap away at the keyboard. Two hours and several drafts later, he printed out his article to show to Uncle Ray next day for his editorial approval.

THE BIG KICK-OFF
by our soccer correspondent

Fenthorpe Forest 13 – 0 Swillsby Swifts

The people of Swillsby will be glad to know that the village has a new junior soccer team to be proud of. The Swifts have been

formed by player-manager Luke Crawford who skippered his men in their first Sunday League match of the season. Unfortunately, there were only ten of them, and such a handicap against the powerful home side proved too much of a disadvantage.

On a hot, dry afternoon, Forest caught fire and got off to a blazing start. They were four goals ahead before Crawford could marshal his troops and restrict the number of chances being created. The spirited Swifts managed to dampen down the flames but were never quite able to put out the fire.

'The final result was a bit flattering to Forest,' said the Swifts' coach afterwards, 'but our team has learnt a few things that can be put to good use in future games.'

The new player-manager was equally philosophical. 'This is only the start,' remarked Luke Crawford. 'There's a long way to go yet and our sights are firmly set on promotion. The soccer season is a marathon, not a sprint, and I'm confident we'll last the distance.'

Let's all wish the lads good luck for the

rest of the season. They're a promising bunch of players.

Luke was quite pleased with his effort, especially keeping up that forest fire analogy for a whole paragraph. He'd also managed to work in three name-checks for himself and made up some encouraging quotes for his players to read when the *Chronicle* was pushed through their letterboxes.

'All good publicity for the Swifts too,' he smiled. 'Now people know we're here, they might come along and watch us play.'

The editor only raised his eyebrows once as he was reading Luke's prose. That was right at the very beginning and he kept them raised in amazement all the way through.

'Hmm, you've got an imaginative style, Luke, I'll say that,' he said tactfully, peering at his nephew over his glasses. 'No-one else would have written this piece quite like you, I'm sure.'

'Thanks, Uncle Ray,' Luke grinned. 'I'm glad you like it.'

'Ye-es, but it may need a little bit of editing. We've only got limited space, you know.'

He persuaded Luke to revise and cut certain sections – mainly those involving the forest fire,

the name-checks and the quotes – and suggested that a few details about the actual game would not go amiss.

Luke felt the final outcome was somewhat duller and less personal, but he was just happy for the present that his work was going to be published. He was determined, though, that his reports on the Swifts' progress during the season would become a regular feature in the *Chronicle*.

And with less editorial interference in future.

Preparations for the Swifts' second match, at home to Westbrooke United, took up most of the final week of the summer holidays.

Luke signed up two more players, younger lads who had just left the primary school, to make up the numbers until he could find better alternatives when they were back at the Comp. He also had the Swifts report for extra training on three afternoons.

Only on the Friday, though, were all twelve players in attendance. Jordan never appeared once and sent a message through Craig that he'd decided to give up football.

'Bang goes the new kit,' groaned Sean. 'Well done, Skipper. That must be one of the shortest careers on record. Didn't take long to put him off the game for life.'

'Even Frosty would have been proud of that,' said Big Ben with a grin. 'One down, only eleven more to go!'

Luke ignored them and tried to keep the mood upbeat. 'We've worked hard this week, men,' he said in praise. 'It's looking good. I'm sure all our efforts will be rewarded with a home victory.'

'You live in cloud-cuckoo-land,' said Sanjay. 'The Swifts have about as much chance of winning a match as you do of winning the Miss Swillsby beauty contest.'

Dazza chipped in. 'I'm not bothered what the final result is, anyway. Just want to have some

96

fun and enjoy a game of footie every week.'

'Same here,' said Titch. 'At least with the Swifts we can have a good kickabout without old Frosty bawling at us.'

Luke shrugged. 'Fine, OK. But it'd still be nice to win, wouldn't it? Try to score more goals than the other team.'

'That's sure gonna take some doing, the rate we let 'em in,' cackled Tubs. 'I mean, look who we've got in goal!'

The scrappy six-a-side game that followed was highlighted, however, by a wonderful goal. Brain cracked the ball on the half-volley from distance and Sanjay never even moved for the shot as it swerved past him.

'Great stuff, Brain!' cried Luke. 'We'll have another one of those from you on Sunday, please.'

The loyal Brain duly obliged. Just before half-time, he opened the Swifts' scoring account in the league with a rasping drive from well outside the Westbrooke penalty area. The ball was still gathering pace as it rocketed into the net.

It was a goal that deserved to win any game. The pity was that the Swifts were 5–0 down at the time.

They'd almost gone into a shock lead in fact

soon after the start when a sliced pass from Sean was deflected to Luke, hovering around the penalty spot. The skipper might as well have been *hoovering* for all the threat that he carried to United's goal.

A rush of adrenalin flooded his system in anticipation of scoring and a big, bold headline in the *Chronicle* swam before his eyes.

CRAWFORD GOAL SINKS UNITED

It must have clouded his vision. Luke's attempt at curling the ball into the corner was accurate in only one respect. The ball swirled away to hit the corner flag rather than the vacant corner of the net. Once his heart had stopped pounding, his rose-tinted commentary described the shot as '*screwing just narrowly wide of the target*'.

After that the visitors took control and gave the Swifts a footballing lesson. The procession of goals was interrupted only by Brain's flash of brilliance until Tubs brought the house down and stopped the show.

Trundling after the ball to collect it from the net after United's ninth goal, he jumped up to swing from the crossbar in the way he'd seen

goalkeepers sometimes do.

'Quit hanging around, Tubs,' sneered Sanjay, cross that he'd let the shot slither through his grasp. 'You look like a fat banana, dangling up there.'

A sharp crack was heard all over the recky. Tubs released his grip just in time and rolled clear as the wooden bar snapped apart, the two jagged, splintered ends sagging down towards the ground.

Everyone gathered round to inspect the damage. 'Have you got another crossbar?' asked the referee.

Uncle Ray went to check in the cabin store and came back shaking his head. 'Sorry, ref. No spares in there, I'm afraid.'

'Well, we can't play on with the bar like that,' he said. 'Even if we managed some sort of temporary repair, it'd be too dangerous. It might collapse again at any time on top of somebody.'

'So what happens now?' asked Luke's dad.

'I'll have to call the game off. Sorry, folks, match abandoned.'

The players and supporters of Westbrooke United were even more sorry.

'C'mon, ref, that's not fair. Can't you award the points to us?' appealed their manager. 'We were going to win easily, anyway.'

'Not in my powers,' the official said. 'The score doesn't count. You'll have to play the game again some time.'

Luke sidled up to his heavyweight defender. 'Well done, Tubs. You've saved us from defeat there,' he whispered. 'I reckon that makes you my *Man of the Match*!'

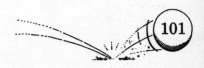

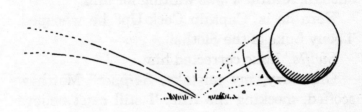

9   Third-Time Lucky?

It felt strange for Luke to be returning to school in September with the football season already underway. Normally he'd have to wait a while yet before the teacher got around to arranging soccer trials – without any guarantee of his ever playing a proper match.

Things had changed. *He* was now the one who picked the team. Even so, with all the games he'd play for the Swifts this season, Luke still hoped that he might improve enough to become a regular for the Comp too!

First, however, he knew he'd have to ride all

the taunts about the Swifts that the likes of Matthew – and possibly even Frosty – were expected to hurl his way. He braced himself as he walked into his new Year 8 classroom. Sure enough, Matthew was waiting for him.

'Here he is, Captain Cock-Up!' he whooped. 'Loony Luke of the Sloths!'

'*Swifts*,' Luke corrected him.

'Oh, sorry, my mistake, *Skipper*!' Matthew scoffed, mocking the title. 'I still can't believe anybody was so stupid as to sign up with you.'

'Watch it, Matt!' cut in Big Ben from the corner of the room.

'You're all mouth, Big Ben,' Matthew sneered. 'I remember the things you were saying before the holidays. Then you go and join the crazy gang!'

'Yeah, and I remember what you said as well.'

'What was that?'

'Promising to do a streak in assembly if Luke ever formed a team. Well, now he's done it – so when are you gonna do it?'

The tables were turned on Matthew. 'A proper team, I meant,' he blustered. 'One that might actually win a game some day. Anybody can get a bunch of donkeys together and put old football shirts on their backs.'

Big Ben's chair scraped across the floor as he

stood up quickly to confront Matthew. Tubs placed a large hand on his shoulder. 'He's not worth the aggro, mate. Teacher will be here any minute. You don't want a detention for fighting first day back, do you?'

Matthew jeered. 'Ah, yes, good old Tubs. Loony Luke's secret weapon when it comes to tactics. As soon as the score comes near to double figures, get the roly-poly man to smash the crossbar!'

'Give it a rest, Matt,' said Jon. 'We know you'll never have the nerve to streak across the hall, so you ain't got the right to criticize them.'

'Huh! Sticking up for your cousin again. I'm surprised you didn't go and join forces with him as well in the end like your dad.'

Jon gave his usual little shrug and half-smile. 'Season's only just begun,' he said. 'Early days yet. We'll have to see how things go.'

It was a casual threat, but enough to shut Matthew up. He didn't want to be the one who caused Jon to desert the Panthers.

'Thanks, Johan,' Luke said to his cousin later. 'Appreciate it. Do you really think you might consider signing for the Swifts one day?'

'Don't hold your breath, Luke,' Jon grinned. 'But you never know . . .'

Luke had to put up with more jibes when the *Chronicle* appeared later that week and people guessed who had written the report of the Forest game. Despite the heavy editing, Luke's style was too distinctive to disguise.

'Wish you hadn't put in some of that stuff, Skip,' said Dazza at their midweek practice session. 'Made us sound well sad. You're not going to do it again, are you?'

'Might do,' said Luke, undeterred.

'Hardly dare think what you'll write if we actually win,' chuckled Tubs. 'We'll all have to go into hiding till the laughter dies down.'

'Just be grateful the *Chronicle* only comes out once a month,' said Mark. 'Luke won't have a chance to describe that crossbar incident!'

Tubs shrugged. 'At least I preserved our unbeaten home record. Played two, won none, lost none, abandoned two!'

'Right, and we're playing Desdale Rangers again on Sunday, only at their place this time,' Luke reminded them. 'They might be a bit too over-confident and we can take advantage of that. Football's a funny game.'

'Not that funny,' Sanjay put in. 'Think I'll take my calculator.'

Sean laughed. 'There's no danger of *us* being over-confident when our own goalie needs a calculator to keep track of how many he lets in!'

'Right, men,' Luke called out to his team. 'All ready?'

He paused to receive their response, which was still not as well rehearsed as he'd like. 'Ready, Skipper,' it came back in staggered timing, accompanied by a few guffaws.

'OK, let's go. Let the Swifts take wing!'

'More like wounded sparrows,' muttered Big Ben.

The team was in the wars again. Two players

were out through illness, Craig and one of the younger lads. And Dazza wasn't feeling too good either. A virus was going around the Comp, explained away by some as being allergic to school.

Whatever it was, the Swifts found out that it had struck the village of Desdale, too, and the Rangers were affected even worse. The ten men of Swillsby were taking on the nine of Desdale.

'These fixtures between us must be cursed,' said Luke's dad as the depleted sides took the field. 'First the floods and now the plague.'

Ray grinned. 'At least it gives our lads more of a chance.'

'Hmm, about as much chance as a turkey of opening his Christmas presents!' grunted his brother.

Luke was far more optimistic. 'This could be third-time lucky, men,' he told them as they gathered in a group before the kick-off. 'A good performance today and we'll be on our way up that league table.'

'Who's he trying to kid?' laughed Sanjay. 'Himself or us?'

'I notice you haven't got your calculator,' Luke said pointedly.

'When I run out of fingers, I'll take off my boots

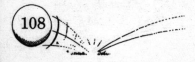

and start counting on my toes,' he replied.

Happily for the Swifts, this was one match that Sanjay wouldn't need to finish barefoot. He found himself on top form, a strange event that did happen from time to time, and he also enjoyed some slices of good fortune.

'Great save!' Luke praised him as Sanjay dived to smother an awkward, low shot that bobbled on the bone-hard goalmouth. 'Got your body right behind that one. Keep it up.'

He did. Shots stuck in his gloves instead of bouncing out, efforts that beat him missed the target too, and when he parried a flashing, near-post header, the ball flipped up on to the crossbar and dropped over.

Sanjay jumped up to give the bar a tap of thanks. 'I'll do that before every game in future,' he decided. 'I need the woodwork on my side.'

It came to his aid once more a few minutes later. This time a post prevented the Swifts from falling behind as a shot was deflected beyond the goalkeeper's reach to hit the upright and bounce away to safety.

The excitement then switched to the other end of the pitch. Totally against any sense of justice, and to everyone's disbelief, the ball was to be seen nestling in the back of the Rangers' net.

Luke had a dual role to play in the goal, both as accidental provider and over-excited commentator. *The skipper's on the ball now, looking to exploit the gaps in the Rangers' defence. He spots Sean moving into space and lays a pin-point pass into his path . . . er . . . into Brain's path instead and the winger's through on goal. He shoots . . . he scores! GOOOAAALLL!!! Brain has put the Swifts in front. The crowd's going crazy . . .'*

Luke certainly was. He leapt on top of Brain as he lay on the ground, soon to be squashed by the arrival of more Swifts. Brain was only just able to wriggle free and scramble to his feet before Tubs steamrollered up to add his weight

to the crush of bodies. It was a narrow escape.

The Rangers' manager was going berserk too. Raging along the touchline, he threatened all manner of punishments if his players didn't get their act together quickly. Ten laps of Desdale Park, including ten press-ups at the end of each one, had a remarkable galvanizing effect.

Rangers moved up a couple of gears just as the visitors seemed to suffer a puncture. The shock of leading was perhaps too much for the Swifts to bear and their performance wilted in the sun as the Rangers launched a series of fierce attacks. The Swifts' cause wasn't helped by Dazza having to leave the field to be sick in the hedge.

The teams were now equal in number and soon the scores were level too. Sanjay's goal was finally breached. His defensive cover was cut to shreds by a rapid sequence of one-touch passing on the edge of the penalty area and Sanjay had no hope of saving the close-range strike.

Nor could he be blamed for the second straight afterwards. The ball spun up off Mark's boot as the centre-back tried to block a shot and the goalkeeper was left clawing at thin air. Even the woodwork could only look on helplessly. The lucky charm had worn off.

By half-time, the score was 3–1 to Rangers and the writing was on the wall for all to read. Even Brain could see that glorious victory was going to elude them, in spite of Luke's efforts during the interval to revive their flagging spirits.

The skipper coaxed and cajoled his team to believe they could still fight their way back into the game, but it was to no avail. Dazza wasn't fit to resume and Big Ben was looking paler by the minute. It was only because some of the Rangers, too, were feeling the strain during the second half that the score didn't mount up alarmingly.

At 5–1, both teams were looking forward to hearing the final whistle and Tubs attempted to use up some time. His method of dropping a subtle hint to the referee was to blast the ball out of play into lunar orbit.

Titch wandered up to him. 'How strong is that crossbar, d'yer reckon, Tubs?' he said cheekily. 'Think it's worth testing it out.'

Tubs shook his head. 'Haven't even got the strength to jump up as high as that now,' he wheezed. 'You should have asked me earlier.'

When the game ended, the Swifts sat together in the centre circle for several minutes to recover and even Luke was temporarily subdued. The disappointment of defeat, after his high expectations, was hard to take.

'For a while there,' he mused, 'I really thought we might do it . . .'

'Never mind, Skipper,' said Brain. 'We nearly grabbed a point.'

'Yeah, that's right, it shows we're starting to improve,' said Big Ben.

Luke could hardly believe his ears. He was normally the one who had to say things like that. Even Sanjay was being supportive for a change.

'Cheer up, Skipper, that was our best effort yet,' said the keeper, clearly in a good mood after his fine display in goal. 'If we could have just held out till half-time . . .'

Tubs chuckled. 'Perhaps you're winning after all, Skipper. Don't give up on us. You see, despite how it might seem at times, we *are* still keen to play.'

'And if you hadn't formed the Swifts, we wouldn't get the chance to,' added Titch.

'Well, er . . . thanks, men,' Luke said, taken aback, before standing up as if he were about to make a speech. Then he launched into one. 'You know me, I'll never give up hope. There's always another day – like next Sunday for instance. Now, in training I want us to work on a few things I've been planning . . .'

'That's what we like about you, Skipper,'

Sanjay interrupted. 'You can always be relied on to bounce back with some daft new ideas. You're a football fruit and nutcase – a fantastic fanatic!'

His teammates burst into tuneless song. *'He's football crazy, he's football mad . . .'*

Luke's face creased up into a silly grin as they sang. Maybe without meaning to, they couldn't possibly have paid him a better compliment!

THE END

*Follow the fortunes of Luke and his teammates in their first season in the next action-packed title in this football series, **Soccer Mad.***

CRAWFORD'S CORNER

Hi! Luke here. Luke Crawford – player-manager, coach and skipper of the newly formed Under-13 Sunday League team, Swillsby Swifts. Newly formed by me, that is, but then I don't really need to tell you that, do I? You've just been reading all about it.

It's early doors yet (as footballers often say in interviews) and I'm confident results will soon improve. The main thing is, we're able to play in a match every week. Like me, most of the lads in the Swifts don't get much of a chance to turn out for the school, and that's why I chose them.

What about you? If you're not getting enough football, you could join one of your local Sunday League clubs and play for them. Or you might fancy trying to start up one of your own. That's what the editor wants me to write about here and she's also asked me to tell you how the game itself began. I know far more about these things than the author, you see.

'Sure,' I said. 'No trouble.' I've got loads of soccer reference books in my bedroom to check out any facts. I think every footie fanatic should know about the history of the game they love.

So are you sitting comfortably? Good. Right, I'll begin at the very beginning . . .

Well, maybe not right back to what historians might call the Pre-season Age. Don't reckon the dinosaurs with their tiny brains would have been very good footballers. It takes at least a bit of intelligence to play the game. (Not that you'd realize, listening to some of those interviews.) I have a pet theory that the reason the dinosaurs became extinct is that they died of boredom because there was no footie to watch on the telly.

And we've no recorded evidence, not even any video *footage* – if you'll pardon the pun – of cavemen kicking rocks around for fun. More likely to be bashing each other over the head with them. In the days before civilization, i.e. before the invention of the soccer boot, footrock as a sport would probably have been too painful.

The earliest known mention of a kind of football is over 2,500 years ago – so long ago it's even before old Frosty was born. Apparently they played a game called Tsu Chu, which roughly translated means 'to kick a ball of stuffed leather'. The Ancient Greeks and Romans also enjoyed their ball games and if

they didn't have anything to stuff their leather with, I suppose the heads of their slaves might have come in handy for a kickabout.

Where the game really caught on in a big way was in medieval England. Whole villages would take part in annual games, often on Shrove Tuesday, followed no doubt by a good feast of pancakes for those still breathing. There must have been some pork going spare too, as the balls were often made from inflated pig-bladders. Not perhaps the kind of object you'd want to handle for too long, even if you were given the chance. Things did tend to cut up a bit rough. Kickin' and gougin', stampin' and bitin', hackin' and trippin', punchin' and well, you name it, were all allowed. Nothing was against the rules because there weren't any rules. No refs either of course. They'd have been lynched.

I know that kind of free-for-all might sound no worse than your average skirmish in the school playground at break. But imagine it being played by huge mobs through country lanes, muddy fields and brooks with the goals miles apart and you get some idea of the scale of the thing.

When football spread into the towns and cities, some people complained about the

noise, just like your neighbours do. In 1314 King Edward II put a stop to such violent revelries in the streets, but the game still survived. It remained popular right through Tudor and Stuart times, and even the old spoilsport Oliver Cromwell failed to ban it for long when he came to power. He was the bloke who had King Charles I's head chopped off after the Civil War – a red card offence if ever there was one. (I don't think even the old 'magic sponge' could have cured a bad injury like that.)

Football soon bounced back, just like balls have a habit of doing, and Samuel Pepys mentioned them in his famous diary. On 3rd January 1665, he wrote about: 'the street being full of footballs, it being a great frost'. Wonder if the Great Plague of that time caused a few games to be postponed?

It wasn't until the nineteenth century, though, that the game began to get more organized. It was played at many public schools and universities by now and Cambridge laid down a set of rules in the 1840s that would sound to us more like rugby. You could still catch the ball but only do kicked passes, throw-ins were one-handed and goals had no restriction in height. (More of my shots would go in if that was still the rule!)

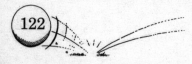

Let me give you some more important dates and details:

1863 – The Football Association was formed for clubs around London, devising more rules. This led to the split with those who wanted to continue handling the ball and they broke away to form the Rugby Union.

N.B. Did you know that the word 'soccer' comes from an abbreviation of AsSOCiation? Neat, eh? The story goes that in 1889 a certain Mr Charles Wreford-Brown said he preferred to play soccer rather than rugger.

1871/72 – each team was limited to eleven players, ten outfielders and a goalkeeper. The F.A. Cup tournament was first staged that season, won by the Wanderers who beat the Royal Engineers 1–0 in the final at Kennington Oval with an attendance of 2,000 people.

N.B. All this kind of information is vital if you want to impress your mates with your in-depth knowledge of soccer trivia.

1888/89 – Formation of the Football League with just twelve clubs in the Midlands and the north of England. Preston North End won the championship in both the first two seasons.

1890 – Scottish and Irish Leagues formed. The rules kept being changed to make the

game more like the one we play today, but they're still messing about with them now, as you know. The main ones were the introduction of crossbars (1875), the two-handed throw-in (1882), nets on goals (1891) and penalty kicks (1892).

Football gradually began to spread abroad to Europe and beyond and now it's the most popular game on the planet. The first World Cup was held in Uruguay, South America, in 1930, even though England didn't join in until 1950 when we lost 1–0 to the U.S.A. So we gave football to the world and now everybody loves to come and play at Wembley, the 'home' of football, and beat us at our own game.

I know the feeling – of losing, that is. But as they say in the Olympics, it's the taking part that counts, not the winning. (Nah, I don't really believe that either!) At least the Swifts have made a start and we've all got to start some-where. You never know where things might lead. Who'd have thought that the riotous sport of medieval times would become the beautiful game graced by the likes of Johan Cruyff?

If you *are* thinking about forming your own team, don't leave it too late like we nearly did. We were lucky. Uncle Ray knows the right

people and managed to pull a few strings for us, know what I mean? It's best if you start planning well in advance of applying to join a local league. You'll need some adults to help, I'm afraid, but they can do all the boring tasks like being secretary and treasurer and suchlike. That leaves you free to concentrate on the job that really matters – out on the pitch.

You'd be totally gobsmacked at how expensive running a club can be. It costs hundreds of pounds a season, so asking some sponsors to support you is a good idea, even if you have to suffer a silly name on the kit they provide. Better than having to wear somebody else's cast-offs like us.

There's tons of other stuff you have to deal with, too, but the League Secretary will explain all that. A local club, library or even your sports teacher – so long as he (or she) is not as grumpy as Frosty – should be able to give you the name of someone to contact for more details.

Best of luck – you'll need it. Enjoy your footie, win or lose, but watch out if you ever come up against the Swifts. We'll lick you!

See ya!

Luke.

ABOUT THE AUTHOR

Rob Childs was born and grew up in Derby. His childhood ambition was to become an England cricketer or footballer – preferably both! After university, however, he went into teaching and taught in primary and high schools in Leicestershire, where he now lives. Always interested in school sports, he coached school teams and clubs across a range of sports, and ran area representative teams in football, cricket and athletics.

Recognizing a need for sports fiction for young readers, he decided to have a go at writing such stories himself and now has more than fifty books to his name, including the popular *The Big Match* series, published by Young Corgi Books.

Rob has now left teaching in order to be able to write full-time. Married to Joy, also a writer, Rob has a "lassie" dog called Laddie and is also a keen photographer.

SOCCER MAD
Rob Childs

'This is going to be the match of the century!'

Luke Crawford is crazy about football. A
walking encyclopedia of football facts and
trivia, he throws his enthusiasm into being
captain of the Swillsby Swifts, a Sunday
team made up mostly of boys like himself –
boys who love playing football but get few
chances to play in real matches.

Luke is convinced that good teamwork and
plenty of practice can turn his side into
winners on the pitch, but he faces a real
challenge when the Swifts are drawn to
play the Padley Panthers – the league
stars – in the first round of the Sunday
League Cup . . .

0 440 863449

CORGI YEARLING BOOKS

ALL GOALIES ARE CRAZY
Rob Childs

*. . . BUT SOME GOALIES ARE MORE
CRAZY THAN OTHERS!*

No-one enjoys keeping goal so much as
Sanjay Mistry – the regular, if un-
predictable, goalie both for the school team
and for the Swillsby Swifts, the Sunday
league team led by soccer-mad Luke
Crawford. But after Sanjay makes a series
of terrible match-losing blunders, Luke
decides that it's time someone else had a
go at playing in goal – himself!

Determined to prove himself as the number
one goalie, Sanjay rises to the challenge
with some outstanding and acrobatic saves.
But Luke's enthusiasm and crazy antics
make him a surprisingly serious rival . . .

0 440 863503

CORGI YEARLING BOOKS